SHOOT FOR
THE HOOP

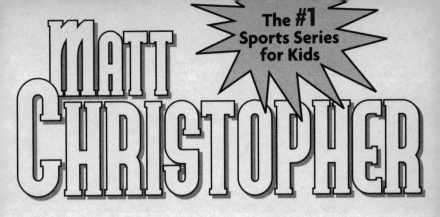

SHOOT FOR
THE HOOP

Little, Brown and Company
Boston   New York   London

To
John and Ann

SHOOT FOR
THE HOOP

1

Rusty Young blew the whistle as hard as he could. The shrill sound pierced the stillness of the night. It was so loud his own ears rang.

"Foul on Perry!" Rusty shouted.

"What?"

The boys on the court stopped moving instantly. The tallest one stared at Rusty, his eyes cold and hard.

"You hit Joey's wrist when you stole the ball from him!" Rusty said. "I saw you!"

He trotted forward across the asphalt of

the lighted outdoor court, took the ball from Perry, and handed it to Joey. "One shot," he said.

He felt Perry's stinging glance. Perry always thought he could get away with anything. Probably because he handled the ball better than any of them and because he was the tallest.

Rusty didn't care. He'd call the fouls if he saw them, just like the referees did in the big games.

Joey stepped to the free-throw line. One of the boys had repainted it just a few weeks ago.

Joey held the ball close to his chest and looked long and hard at the basket. Players stood on each side of the free-throw lane, watching him. Rusty watched him, too. He couldn't help smiling a little. Every time Joey tried a foul shot, his mouth hung wide open.

Joey shot. The ball hit the backboard, bounced back, and fluttered through the net.

"Nice shot!" somebody yelled.

Joey's mouth snapped shut like a trap, and he grinned.

Jim Bush caught the ball as it dropped from the basket. He stepped near the fence at one side of the backboard and passed the ball to Perry. Perry dribbled it downcourt.

Rusty followed him. For a split second, he found himself admiring Perry's skillful ball handling. He saw that Cam Mullins was looking for a pass; he wanted to shout to Perry that Cam was wide open.

Then he reminded himself to concentrate on monitoring the game. As referee, it was his job to be sure both sides were playing fairly, not to help one team score against the other. Still, he was disappointed when Perry drove for the hoop instead of passing to Cam. He could tell Cam was, too.

More than anything, Rusty wanted to be on the court as a player. And he would have been, too, if it hadn't been for something that had happened to him nine months ago.

School had just started up again. Each afternoon, Rusty and his buddies met at the outdoor basketball court at the park for a four-on-four pickup game. Rusty was playing forward, as usual, with Joey and Cam at guard and Perry in the other forward slot.

It was during a five-minute break that it happened. Rusty had been feeling odd all game, but suddenly he knew something wasn't right. Unlike the other boys, whose breathing had returned to normal, Rusty couldn't seem to catch his breath. The air was cooling as dusk fell, yet Rusty was sweating hard. But it wasn't until someone handed him a bottle of water to drink from — even though he wasn't thirsty at all — that he noticed his hands were shaking uncontrollably.

The last thing he remembered hearing before he passed out was Joey asking him if he was all right.

He woke up in a hospital bed. His parents were at his side. Both looked as though they had been crying. Rusty was about to ask what was wrong when Dr. Leonard walked into the room, pulled a chair up in front of him, and looked him in the eye.

"How're you feeling, Rusty?" he asked.

"Weird," Rusty replied. "What's going on?"

Dr. Leonard took a deep breath. "Rusty, there's just no way to tell you other than straight out. You have diabetes."

Rusty blinked. He'd heard that word before. He wasn't sure what it meant. But he could tell from his parents' faces that it was something bad.

The doctor tried to explain. "Diabetes is a common disease that affects many, many people, young and old. Basically diabetes is caused when a hormone called insulin doesn't work right. When this happens, your body cannot correctly process the food you eat — especially sugary foods like candy and sweets — into energy."

Dr. Leonard looked solemnly at Rusty. "When your body has too much or too little insulin in it, you have a very bad reaction. That's what happened to you, Rusty; you lost consciousness on the basketball court because you had too much insulin in your system. The good news is, now that we have a diagnosis, you should never have to go through an experience like that again.

"The bad news is that there is no cure for

diabetes. However, it *can* be controlled by regulating your diet, checking your blood sugar level, and taking insulin shots every day. I know it sounds scary, but most people diagnosed with diabetes live very normal lives. Once you learn how the routine works, you should have no problem."

And that was that.

Now, months later, Rusty was used to the routine. He had learned what he could and couldn't eat, and how to monitor any changes in how he felt. He knew he had to carry a packet of candy with him at all times and that he should pop a piece in his mouth if he started to feel bad. Just in case, he wore a medical alert tag on a chain around his neck to let people know he was a diabetic.

But one thing he couldn't face learning was how to give himself insulin shots. He knew he couldn't depend on his parents to do it for him forever; besides, it was clear it wasn't easy for them to do, either. His mother still took a deep breath before she stuck the needle into his arm.

But he just didn't feel ready to do it himself. Not yet.

There were other problems, too. The way his friends treated him at first, for example — as if he would break if they even touched him! The pitying look on his teachers' faces when he told them wasn't much better. Fortunately, as the first weeks went by, nearly everyone started treating him normally again.

But not everything was all right. Except for not giving himself shots, Rusty felt pretty much in control of his disease. But his mother had forbidden him to play basketball.

"I just don't know what that amount of exercise will do to you," she had said. "What if you had another insulin reaction on the court? I don't think I could go through that again."

Rusty didn't give up, though. Eventually his parents had agreed that he could act as referee at the pickup games. Depending on how that went, they'd talk again about his playing.

So now, instead of pulling off his shirt to join the "skins" team, Rusty jogged slowly up and down the sidelines, watching for fouls — and spotting opportunities for strong offensive plays he was sure he wouldn't have missed if he had been playing.

2

Rusty watched Perry dribble toward the basket. Cam Mullins was guarding Perry closely. Quick as a wink, Perry dribbled past him and broke for the basket. He went up, bounced the ball against the backboard, and scored two points.

The ball dropped to the asphalt, and Rusty caught it on the bounce. He tossed it to a boy waiting to take it out. Then he saw a movement in the shadows and paused to get a better look.

A man was leaning against the doorway of

the fenced-in court. Rusty recognized him in an instant, although he had never spoken to him. His name was Alec Daws. His father had recently purchased the grocery store in Cannerville. They were still a little like strangers.

Alec stepped onto the court. A wide grin spread across his face.

"Keep playing," he said. "Don't stop because of me."

As usual, Rusty was struck by how tall Alec was. He even towered over Perry, who was almost five feet ten! Then his gaze fell upon Alec Daws's left hand.

For the first time, Rusty noticed that Alec was missing two fingers. But before he had a chance to react to that discovery, Perry called to him to get the game going again.

The boys played awhile longer. Rusty blew the whistle a couple of times when he thought a foul had been made. Both times the boys on whom Rusty made the call yelled at him. And both times Rusty's face turned red.

"Here, Alec," he said at last, holding the ball out toward the tall onlooker. "You ref."

"No. You're doing all right," said Alec Daws.

"Good idea!" Perry Webb exclaimed. "Come on, Alec! Ref for us!"

Alec Daws smiled, shrugged, and accepted the ball from Rusty.

Rusty went to the bench at the side of the court and sat down. The boys played more carefully now that Alec was refereeing. But while Rusty watched, an ache started inside him. An ache to be on the court, to run. An ache to scramble after the ball, to dribble it, and to shoot for the basket.

After a while, when the action was taking

place near the farther basket, he stood up and slipped through the door.

He was glad the darkness of the night hid his face when he glanced back over his shoulder. Not that it mattered — no one seemed to notice he was gone.

Rusty walked across the cracked cement sidewalk alongside the street. Behind him, he could hear loud calls and the sounds of running, thumping feet.

He walked slowly, breathing in the cool night air. A high moon hung like a glowing crystal ball in the sky. It was about eight o'clock. His mom and dad expected him home soon, anyway.

He got to thinking about his future. It looked very dim. Alec Daws had taken an interest in the boys' playing basketball. He might be coming to the court more often now. No doubt he understood the game well. At least, well enough to know how to referee.

All at once Rusty didn't like Alec Daws. He didn't like him at all. Alec had come and taken away from him the one thing he was able to do: referee.

The evening was so quiet, Rusty could hear the soft whisper of the creek water to his left. He walked alongside the concrete wall and watched the moonlit water glisten like patches of silver. He reached the bridge, crossed it, and started down the paved road.

Ahead, on the left, was the Dawses' grocery store. A dim yellow light beamed out from its big window. The store was closed.

Rusty looked up at the hill behind the store. It was steep, covered with pine trees, elms, and oaks. On top of the hill he could see the outline of a house. Other houses were up there, out of his view. One of them was his.

Rusty paused. He could continue on his way home by taking the road. It led past the store, then wound around the hill and up to the houses. But now he wanted to take the shortcut. He would climb the steep hill.

He walked behind the store, reached the bottom of the hill, and began climbing. He discovered that the dark tree-shadows made it hard to see. The footing was difficult, too. Slippery wet leaves and pine needles covered the ground.

He ducked beneath the low branches of a tree. Suddenly his ankle twisted beneath him and he fell to the ground! He started to roll down the steep slope but managed to catch hold of a small sapling before he slid too far.

He began to climb again, trying to avoid

the scrub brush that snagged at the legs of his sweatpants. By the time he was three fourths up the hill, he was breathing harder than he had for weeks. Drops of perspiration trickled down the sides of his face.

Finally he reached the top. He found a spot where he could easily climb over the stone wall that separated the street from the hill's slope. He started to walk the last leg to his house when he heard his name being called.

"Rusty! Rusty, wait for me!"

Joey's voice rang out. Rusty could see him running swiftly toward him.

"Rusty, where'd you go? The game broke up a few minutes after Alec Daws showed up. But when I looked for you, you had disappeared!"

Rusty was about to reply, but Joey interrupted him.

"Hey, are you okay? You — you look kind of funny, and you're sweating a lot," he said.

"I took the shortcut home. It tired me out more than I thought it would, I guess. But except for a twisted ankle, I'm fine." Yet when he raised his hand to wipe the sweat from his brow, he saw he was trembling. He knew from the look on his face that Joey saw it, too.

Warning bells went off in his head. He was sweating, his breathing was shallow, and his hands were shaking. It might just be from his climb up the hill — or he could be having an insulin reaction!

Dr. Leonard had told him that if he thought he was having a reaction, it was better to eat a small piece of candy than to ignore the symptoms. Rusty fumbled in his sweatshirt pocket for the packet of hard candies he kept there.

But his pocket was empty!

"Joey!" he said frantically. "I — I think I may be in trouble. Can you help me get home fast?"

Joey understood instantly. He crouched down, pointed to his back, and said, "Hop on. I'll piggyback you home before you know it!"

3

Less than a minute later, Joey was helping Rusty through his front door. Rusty's father was on the phone, but when he saw the boys, he hung up hastily.

"Rusty, what's wrong?"

"Dad, I think I may be having an insulin reaction. Could you get me a glass of orange juice?" Rusty sank weakly into a chair. His father disappeared into the kitchen. He reappeared a second later with the juice.

Rusty drank, holding the glass as steadily as his shaking hand would allow. Slowly the juice took effect. A few minutes later, he was feeling almost normal.

His dad took the glass from him and knelt down. "What happened?"

Rusty explained. "I must have dropped my candy when I fell," he finished.

When Rusty's mother heard the story, her forehead furrowed with worry.

"You're just lucky Joey was there to help you," she said. "But I'm more convinced than ever that playing basketball isn't a good idea. In fact," she added, "I'm not even sure that you should referee anymore."

Rusty's heart sank. He knew there would be no arguing with his mother now. But somehow he'd show her that if she let him play again, he wouldn't let what happened tonight happen again.

For the rest of the week, Rusty stayed away from the basketball court. Joey stopped over on Friday to fill him in on what was happening.

"Alec Daws has been coaching us," he said, his voice full of enthusiasm. "He split us into new teams because he said we needed to get used to playing with different people. We have seven people, so we play three-on-three, with one person sitting out.

"But the best thing," he continued, "is that Alec thinks we're good enough to play in the summer league when school lets out next month! It's the real thing, with uniforms, referees, scoring, even a championship series, not just the pickup games like we played last summer. Isn't that great?"

Rusty didn't say a word out loud, just nodded. But inside, he knew he wanted to be a part of that team. It wouldn't be easy.

After Joey left, Rusty called Dr. Leonard. The doctor had been told about his recent "low." While he had been concerned, he had praised Rusty for recognizing his symptoms and taking the proper action.

On the phone now, Rusty asked Dr. Leonard about the effects of exercise on his diabetes.

"Exercise naturally lowers the blood sugar level, Rusty," Dr. Leonard replied. "Unless you take precautions, it could mean you end up with too much insulin in your system. That's what happened the other day when you climbed that steep hill after running up and down the court, refereeing. The best thing to do if you *know* you're going to be exercising hard is to have your parents give you a little extra starch with lunch. That will give your sugar level enough of a boost to tide you over. But if you're just going to be shooting hoops, you shouldn't need to change anything."

"Thanks, Doc," Rusty said. "That's just what I wanted to hear!"

"Just be careful, Rusty. Make sure you have candy with you. With diabetes, any change in your routine can be a little risky."

"I'll be careful," Rusty promised. Then he took a deep breath and asked the question he'd been putting off since the phone call began. Actually, to be honest, it was something he'd been putting off for a lot longer.

"Dr. Leonard, do you think I could come to your office this weekend and learn how to give myself my insulin injections? I — I want to surprise my parents, so I'd like to come alone."

Dr. Leonard didn't reply right away.

What if he doesn't think I'm ready? Rusty worried. What if he insists that Mom and Dad be there? How will I explain to them why I want to learn about injecting myself all of a sudden?

Before he could come up with answers

to any of these questions, Dr. Leonard spoke.

"Sorry to keep you waiting, Rusty," he said. "I had to check my calendar of appointments. Why don't you stop by around ten o'clock on Saturday? Plan on spending a few hours here at least. This isn't something you're going to learn to do quickly."

Rusty thanked the doctor and promised he'd be there. And despite the doctor's warning, he promised himself that by the end of the session, he'd be a pro at giving himself shots.

That evening, after his regular insulin shot and a tasty dinner, Rusty asked his parents if he could go out for a while. He told himself he wasn't deceiving them — he just didn't tell them where he wanted to go. They said yes.

Armed with the knowledge that just shooting hoops would be okay, he changed into his sweat suit, laced up his high-top basketball sneakers, and dug his ball out of the back of his closet. Then he walked to the outdoor court. But first he made sure he had zipped a pack of candy into his pocket.

To Rusty's relief, no one else was on the court. It felt strange to be there alone, but after a moment or two, the strangeness wore off.

He dribbled his basketball, switching from one hand to the other as he made his way slowly down the court. He stopped and shot. Missed! He caught the bouncing ball, spun, shot again. This time the ball rebounded hard off the backboard and ricocheted like a rocket right back at him.

Rusty moved to a different spot on the court. He took careful aim this time and was rewarded with a *swish!* from the net as the ball passed cleanly through.

But that was the last decent shot he made for the next ten minutes. His shots were either too short or too far to one side of the hoop. He tried jump shots, layups, even a hook shot or two, but it was no good.

Anger built up inside him. A year ago, he would have made most of those shots without a second thought! But a year ago, he didn't have diabetes. Why did he have to be different from other boys? *Why did it have to happen to him?*

"Hello!" a voice behind him said.

He dropped the ball. He spun and almost lost his balance.

"Oh! Hi!" he said. His heart thumped. "Hi, Mr. Daws!"

4

I saw you pass by the store with the basketball," said Alec. "I thought you were coming here. Practicing shots?"

"I guess so," said Rusty.

Alec came forward. He walked gracefully despite his towering height. A smile warmed his gray eyes. Then a little frown appeared on his forehead.

"Aren't you the boy who was refereeing the ball game here a few nights ago?"

Rusty nodded. He was really nervous. Boy, this guy was tall!

"Bet you didn't like it when I took over your job, did you?" Alec Daws said.

Rusty looked away. He shrugged. "I — I didn't mind," he said.

Alec Daws gave Rusty a half-smile. "Don't tell me that," he said. "What's your name? Mine's Alec Daws. You can call me Alec."

"My name's Ronald Young," said Rusty. "Everybody calls me Rusty. Because of my hair."

Alec laughed.

Rusty's gaze fell upon Alec's left hand — the one with the missing fingers. After a quick glance, he looked up guiltily. He hadn't meant to stare; it wasn't polite. He hoped Alec hadn't noticed. After all, if he was going to try to be on Alec's team, it would be better to start off on the right foot.

"Go ahead," said Alec. "Let's see you hit one from here."

Rusty turned and looked at the basket. He stood near the middle of the court. He had no chance of even hitting the backboard from here. He began to dribble, then stopped. He stood frozen, his face turning red.

"What's the matter, Rusty?"

"N-nothing," he said. He shot. The ball fell far short.

So much for starting off on the right foot, he thought miserably.

Suddenly Alec swept past him. He caught the bouncing ball with one hand — the right hand — and dribbled it to the side. He stopped, held the ball up in both hands, then shot at the basket. Rusty noticed that Alec had used his left hand to guide the ball up in front of him. When he shot, he used only his right hand.

The ball arced beautifully and sank through the hoop.

Rusty stared. What a shot!

"Now you try it, Rusty," Alec said. He caught the ball and tossed it to Rusty.

Rusty dribbled slowly toward the basket, then stopped and looped a shot. The ball banged against the rim and dropped to the ground.

"Go after it!" said Alec.

Rusty did. He reached the ball, tried to make a quick shot, and missed. Once more his face flushed.

Alec caught the ball, dribbled toward him, and grinned.

"Guess I'm a little out of practice," Rusty said weakly.

"Just take it easy," said Alec. "You rushed the ball too fast. I have a suggestion. Go over to that corner. Inside the playing area."

Rusty went to the corner. Alec bounced the ball to him.

"Shoot," said Alec, "then chase after the ball, and shoot from the opposite side."

Rusty shot. He missed, went after the ball, and shot it from the other corner.

"Make that your goal," said Alec. "Every time you come here, practice those corner shots. You'll start hitting, and someday you'll be a corner-shot artist."

Rusty grinned. "Okay," he said.

He and Alec took turns shooting at the basket. Rusty saw how gracefully Alec moved, how quickly he dribbled, how smoothly he made his layups.

"Did you ever play on a team, Alec?" Rusty asked.

"In high school and college," said Alec. "Until I hurt my hand."

Rusty's eyes widened. "Hurt your hand playing basketball?"

"Oh, no. I worked on a farm during my summer vacation a few years ago and did it on a corn husker. That finished me." Alec stood near the middle of the court now.

He aimed for the basket and shot. The ball hit the backboard and bounced into the net.

"I have diabetes," Rusty blurted out.

"I know," said Alec. He took another shot, then headed for the doorway. "Well, I'd better get back to the store. Keep shooting, Rusty!"

"Thanks for coming, Alec!" Rusty said.

Five minutes after Alec left, Cam Mullins and Perry Webb showed up.

"Well, look who's here!" cried Perry. "What are you doing, Rusty?"

"Practicing corner shots," replied Rusty. "Alec Daws was just here. He told me to keep at it and maybe I'll become a corner-shot artist."

Perry and Cam exchanged a glance. Then Perry said, "But you're sick! Why bother practicing? I mean, you don't expect to *play*, do you?"

Rusty's lips tightened. He took his ball and started toward the gate.

"Wait!" said Cam. "Stick around. Let's shoot some hoops for a while."

Rusty paused, then turned back. I'll show them! he thought with determination. *Alec* thinks I can play, or else he wouldn't have suggested I learn the corner shot!

They took turns shooting at the basket. Rusty's shots seldom hit. But he did as Alec had suggested. He kept shooting from the corners. Maybe someday he would get good at it.

Maybe.

5

Saturday morning at ten o'clock on the dot, Rusty was sitting in Dr. Leonard's office. Three hours later, he was on his way home, going over in his head everything he had just learned.

Make sure the skin is clean. Firmly pinch about an inch of skin on the thigh. Hold the syringe and needle firmly between the fingers and place the thumb on the plunger. Stick the needle deep into the skin at a seventy-five degree angle, and slowly push the plunger down. Pull the needle out carefully.

It all sounded easy enough.

But he knew it wouldn't be easy the first time he picked up the syringe needle for real. Still, he felt more prepared to try it now than he ever had before.

After lunch, Rusty called Joey. He found out the boys were meeting at the court at two o'clock. "Alec might not be there, though, so we could just play a little three-on-three or maybe four-on-four, if you're up for it?"

Rusty hung up the phone and sat in the quiet kitchen, thinking about what Joey had said. Then, with a determined look in his eye, he changed into his sweats and walked down the hill toward the basketball court.

He hadn't told his parents where he was going. He'd just left a note saying he was with Joey. He pushed his guilty feelings aside. With his newfound confidence for giving himself injections, he was more determined than ever to be a part of Alec Daws's basketball team.

Only three boys, including Joey, were at the court when Rusty arrived. Joey clapped him on the back and said he'd missed seeing "ol' Carrot-top" on the court.

Rusty grinned and playfully punched Joey in the arm. "Feels good to be here again," he said.

Within fifteen minutes, all seven boys who had been coming regularly to play basketball were present. Rusty made eight.

Perry Webb took control of the situation.

"Okay, let's team up the way Alec asked us to. Joey, you and Ted are with me. Cam, you take Bud and Mark. Jim, you'll be our sub." Perry paused, then looked at Rusty. "Ready, ref?" he asked.

Rusty flushed. But before he could say

anything, Joey spoke up. "Rusty's here to play, Perry. That means we can go four-on-four — just like old times. We'll take him on our team, and Jim can go with Cam, Bud, and Mark."

Perry was silent for a moment. Then he said, "Yeah, sure. Well, let's get warmed up!"

For the first time in a long time, Rusty joined in the drills — three-man weaves, rapid passing, and layup shots. Many of his shots came close, but few went in. His passing was accurate, though.

"Did you know Alec has to send in our names to the summer league by the end of next week?" asked Perry. "He called me last night to remind me to bring my permission form today."

Rusty was holding the ball, ready to shoot. Now he looked at Perry.

"Permission form?"

37

"Yeah, everyone has to have their parents sign one before Alec can add them to the roster. I guess he called because he knows how much I want our team to be a part of the league."

Rusty suddenly wondered if his parents would sign a permission form. They didn't even know he still wanted to play basketball!

"Come on, Rusty!" yelled Cam. "Let go of the ball!"

Rusty shot. He threw far short. Cam caught the ball on a bounce, broke fast for the basket, and laid it up neatly.

"He told me the games will start right after school gets out," Perry went on. "Boy, will that be fun!"

I wonder, thought Rusty. I wonder if I'll be part of that fun.

As if he had read his thoughts, Perry met Rusty's eyes and said, "I don't know if you'll be on the team, Rusty. I mean, you only just started practicing. And with your disease and all, well, I don't think Alec would want you on the team. But maybe he'll let you keep score or something."

Rusty's heart sank. What if Perry was right? What if Alec Daws had just been nice to him the other day because he felt sorry for him?

6

A booming voice interrupted Rusty's thoughts. "Is that my up-and-coming corner-shot man I see on the court?"

Rusty spun. Alec Daws was striding toward them. To Rusty's surprise, Dr. Leonard was with him. Alec smiled.

"I had a feeling you'd wind up here today, Rusty. So I took the liberty of asking Dr. Leonard to join us. He's been filling me in on the harrowing adventures you were having this morning. Sounds like you're just the kind of go-getter we want on this team. If

Dr. Leonard agrees that you're physically able to play, all you'll need to do is have your parents sign this permission form."

Shooting Dr. Leonard a grateful look, Rusty took the permission form from Alec and zipped it carefully into his backpack. Although he was sure he would be fine, he felt better knowing the doctor would be right there if anything happened to him. After all, Rusty fully expected to play hard this afternoon!

Alec called for attention. "I've got a new offensive play I'd like to outline, so listen up. I forgot my blackboard, so we'll have to use live bodies to demonstrate it. Cam and Bud, take up the guard positions. Perry'll be our center. Mark and Jim will be our forwards." Alec glanced at Rusty for one brief moment, then continued. "The rest of you watch closely and learn."

Alec told Cam and Bud to take up positions on either side of the center circle at half court. He put Mark and Jim a few yards to the left and right of the foul line. Perry was at the top of the key.

Alec handed the ball to Cam.

"Okay, here's how it goes. Cam, you feed the ball to Perry. If you're being guarded closely, think about making that a bounce pass." Cam bounced a pass to Perry. "Okay, now, Bud, while Cam is passing, you cut for the basket. Look for the quick pass from Perry on the way by him. If he makes the pass, you can either take the shot from the top corner of the key or drive for the hoop."

Cam moved as Alec indicated. Alec stopped Perry just as he was about to make the pass.

"Perry, if you can't make the pass to Bud, look for Mark. He'll be cutting across the middle of the key from right to left. Think about hitting him when he's closest to you since there could be a lot of defensive players around — you don't want the pass to be picked off!"

Mark shuffled across the key. This time, Alec let Perry pass. Mark caught the ball, then waited for Alec's instructions.

"Mark, you'll shoot if you can, then take a few steps in and be ready for a rebound. Perry, Bud, and Jim should all be moving in, too. Cam, you hold back, ready to run down-court for defense just in case we don't get a hoop. Okay, shall we give it a try?"

The first time they moved through the play, it was a disaster. Cam fed the ball to Mark instead of Perry. Bud was so busy looking for a pass that he crashed into Jim. But after a few more run-throughs, they were moving like clockwork.

Alec blew his whistle.

"Well, it's easy enough to do when you don't have someone guarding you. Let's see if you can remain as calm when there are more bodies on the court."

The three remaining boys, Rusty, Ted, and Joey, trotted onto the court. Alec removed his whistle and took a position next to Ted. Eyes twinkling, he pointed to Dr. Leonard. "We seem to be a player short. Would the good doctor like to participate?"

With a laugh, Dr. Leonard agreed.

When the first string seemed to get the hang of the drill, Alec had the three boys on defense change places with three offensive players. He put Rusty in at guard and handed him the ball.

"Okay, Rusty, let's see how well you listen."

Rusty dribbled a few times, checking to

be sure his team was ready, then fired off a pass to Ted, his center. Out of the corner of his eye, he saw Joey and Perry streak toward the basket, looking for the pass from Ted. But Dr. Leonard and Alec Daws decided to double-team Ted so tightly that he couldn't get the pass off.

Rusty didn't think. He just moved.

"Pass back! Pass back!" he called. Ted pivoted and bounced the ball back to him.

Rusty caught the ball and dribbled straight for the outside corner. Cam lunged out to cover him, leaving Joey wide open. With a graceful, catlike move, Rusty faked a shot. Cam leapt — and Rusty bounced a pass around him to Joey!

Joey was so surprised, he almost didn't catch it. But a moment later, he had laid it up for an easy bucket.

"A good improvisation, Rusty, that led to

two more points for your side." Rusty flushed with pride at Alec's praise. "Remember, guys," Alec continued, "good basketball teams have players who can think on their feet. The defense may not always let you work the offense the way you learned it. It's important to be able to spot options quickly and act on them."

Alec glanced at his watch. "Okay, that's it for today. Can everyone make it tomorrow?" The boys all nodded. "Good, I'll see you then."

Rusty hadn't felt so good in months. Then, as he gathered up his gear, he remembered the permission form tucked in his backpack. Suddenly his good mood fell. He had been enjoying himself so much, he'd pushed that burning problem aside: How was he going to get his parents to sign that form? They didn't even know he was playing basketball!

7

Rusty and Joey headed for their neighborhood together after practice. Rusty had just said good night to Joey and started up his driveway when he heard a car horn toot behind him. It was Alec Daws.

Alec parked the car and got out. "Rusty, since I was in the area, I thought you might like me to be on hand to answer any questions your folks have about the team. Okay by you?"

Rusty nodded uncertainly. He hadn't made up his mind how he was going to approach his parents about playing basketball. Now, with Alec at his side, he had no choice but to plunge right in the minute he walked through the door.

But when he stepped into the house, he found a surprise waiting for him.

"Well, aren't you going to give your big sister a hug?" a voice asked with a laugh.

"Marylou!" Rusty exclaimed. "Why aren't you at college?"

Marylou scooped him into her arms for a big hug. "I'm home for summer vacation, you ninny. Didn't you read my last letter?"

Rusty shook his head. The letter was stuck on the refrigerator, but he just never had gotten around to reading it.

"Oh, well, never mind," she said. She gave him one last pat on the back, then turned to Alec. "Rusty, who's your friend?"

Alec introduced himself, putting out his

right hand. Marylou shook it and smiled. For a second, her eyes flitted over his left hand, but she said nothing. Alec smiled back warmly.

"Are Mom and Dad home?" Rusty asked.

Marylou shook her head, then leaned toward Rusty and sniffed.

"Rusty, why don't you grab a quick shower before they get home?" she suggested, then added, "I'll keep Alec company while you do."

As he headed upstairs, Rusty realized there might be a way to prove to his parents that he was ready to play basketball. And Marylou had unknowingly given him the chance to get everything he needed together.

Ten minutes later, he was ready. His parents had come home while he was in the shower. He could hear them talking and laughing with Marylou and Alec. Rusty snuck down the back stairs into the kitchen.

When he had arranged everything he needed, he called his parents, Alec, and Marylou into the kitchen.

Laid out on the kitchen table were Rusty's daily records of his insulin shots and his blood sugar levels. There was also a bottle of insulin, a syringe, and a brand-new disposable needle. Rusty was wearing a pair of shorts and a T-shirt.

When everyone was in the kitchen, Rusty cleared his throat.

"Mom, Dad, it's time for my nightly insulin shot, isn't it?"

Mr. and Mrs. Young exchanged a glance, then nodded.

"Would you please make sure I've filled the syringe properly?" Rusty asked. He fastened the needle onto the syringe, turned the bottle of insulin upside down, and stuck the needle through the cap. Carefully he pulled back on the plunger. When he thought he had drawn the right amount of medicine into the syringe, he pulled the needle free and handed it to his mother.

She checked the level, nodded, and took a step toward Rusty, ready to give him his shot.

"No, Mom," Rusty said. "Tonight it's my turn."

Before she could say anything, Rusty took the needle from her. He took a seat on a kitchen chair and found the spot on his thigh Dr. Leonard and he had agreed would be a good place to try.

Giving his parents a quick smile, Rusty pinched his skin — and carefully but confidently jabbed the needle in and depressed the plunger!

It all went as smooth as pie — except that his mother fainted.

When she had recovered, she shook her head in wonder. "Rusty, when did you learn how to do that?" she asked.

Rusty explained about his long session with Dr. Leonard.

"Who knew our son was so brave — or his mother so chickenhearted?" Mom said when he was finished. They all laughed.

Then Alec stepped forward. "Rusty, don't you have something else to show your parents?"

Rusty nodded slowly. He reached behind him, pulled the permission form out of his knapsack, and handed it to his mother.

All of a sudden, her expression grew dark. "Rusty, you know how I feel about your playing basketball. After what happened —"

"Mrs. Young, Rusty forgot to mention that

the doctor's office wasn't the only place Rusty saw Dr. Leonard today," Alec cut in. "The doctor was with us on the basketball court, too. I asked him to be there. After practice, he gave me his opinion about Rusty's becoming part of the team."

Rusty held his breath.

"He said he thought it would be one of the best things Rusty could do."

Rusty grinned — but his smile faded when he glanced at his mother. She looked angry.

"I think I know what's best for my son," she said tightly. And with that, she left the room.

8

Rusty's father was the first one to break the stunned silence.

"Alec, I need to talk with Rusty in private. Marylou, could you walk Alec to the door?"

The two left quietly. Dad turned to Rusty and smiled.

"I'm proud of you, son," he said. "And if it makes you feel any better, I agree with Dr. Leonard and Alec that you should be a part of that team.

"But," he added when Rusty looked up hopefully, "we have to convince your mother, too, before you can play."

"How?" Rusty asked.

Before Dad could answer, there was a soft tap at the kitchen door. Alec walked back in, with Rusty's mother and sister close behind.

"I'm sorry to barge in again," Alec said. "But there was something I wanted you all to know about me."

Alec held up his left hand, the one with the missing fingers.

"When I got hurt a few years ago, I ended my basketball career. No one told me I had to stop playing. I just decided it for myself. So I sat on the sidelines and watched as my team won the play-offs. I know now that it was a mistake to quit. I love playing basketball — I don't think I knew how much until I started coaching Rusty and the other boys of Cannerville. I know I'm a good coach, but because I took myself out of the game without giving myself a chance, I'll never know if I could have been an equally good player."

He laid a hand on Rusty's shoulder.

"I wish I had been more like Rusty. You should have seen him on the court today. He's smart, and he's willing to take the risks — risks that go beyond the physical challenges of coping with diabetes every day."

Alec looked at Rusty's parents solemnly.

"Can you imagine what it's like to suddenly be treated like an invalid by people you've horsed around with all your life? I can. But I bet I could have made them treat me like just another one of the guys if I hadn't treated *myself* like an invalid. Rusty's the only one who can prove to himself — and his teammates — that he is just as valuable a player now as before he was diagnosed. I sure hope you give him that chance."

With a final glance at Rusty, Alec turned and left.

Dinner was quiet that night. But afterward, Rusty could hear his parents murmuring in the kitchen. Once his mother's voice rose sharply. Rusty and Marylou looked at each other. Marylou shrugged, then smiled encouragingly before returning to the book she was reading.

A few minutes later, his parents emerged from the kitchen. Rusty noticed his father was carrying the family photo album.

His mother sank into the easy chair and looked Rusty in the eye.

"Your father has been reminding me how much you loved to play basketball before the diabetes. With all the changes and adjustments you've been through in the past months, I guess I just figured that had changed, too. But it hasn't, has it?"

Rusty shook his head. "I feel like my old self when I'm out there, Mom," he said. "And most of the guys treat me like they used to, not like I'm sick."

Mrs. Young pulled Rusty to her and gave him a big hug. "Then I'm not going to stand in your way! Where's that permission form?"

Rusty's eyes shone with happiness. A moment later, the signed permission form was safely zipped into his backpack.

Rusty could scarcely believe it. He spent the rest of the night on the phone with Joey, telling him the good news and talking about the upcoming summer league.

But one thing nagged in his brain. It had been so long since he had played basketball regularly, what if he had lost all his skill? He would have a uniform and be part of the team, but what if he spent every game sitting on the bench?

What if his diabetes kept him from being the kind of player he used to be?

9

Over the next week and a half, Rusty was too busy memorizing plays and finishing up with the last days of school to worry too much about his playing.

The team met regularly for after-school practices. Rusty still started out on defense, but he was shooting better every day. He hoped he'd get a chance to show Alec what he could really do.

Then one practice, Alec Daws made a slight change in the usual starting line-up. He had just finished outlining a new play on his blackboard, showing how the offensive *x*'s were to move. Even though he knew he'd be playing defense before he got his chance on offense, Rusty paid close attention.

Then Alec surprised them. Bud and Cam went in as guards, and Joey and Perry as center and forward — but instead of putting Mark in as the second forward, Alec told Rusty to take that position.

Mark looked surprised but switched to defense good-naturedly.

Alec said no more, just blew his whistle to start the five-on-three play.

Bud dribbled the ball down to half-court, with Cam jogging a pass-length away. Perry took up position at the top of the key. Joey hopped from foot to foot at the side of the key, ready for the play to begin.

Rusty stood uncertainly on the other side

of the key. His mind was racing. He thought he knew this play backward and forward — but as a guard, not as a forward. What was the forward supposed to *do*?

Suddenly an image of the blackboard Alec used to detail the plays popped into his head. He tried to zero in on the forward's *x* mark. There, clear as day, was a chalk-drawn arrow showing him how his position was supposed to move.

In a flash, Rusty cut across the key. Once he was in the paint, he pivoted sharply. Now he was just outside the lower corner of the key on the opposite side of the court.

Perry called his name, then bounced a pass to him. Rusty caught it easily. Without hesitation, he shot the ball.

Swish! A clean bucket that barely touched the rim!

Before the next play, Alec switched some

players around again. Now Perry was on defense and Ted was in at center. Rusty took Joey's position, and Mark came in as the other forward.

Even Bud and Cam swapped places, so Bud dribbled the ball downcourt.

This time, though, the offense messed up. Rusty and Cam collided in the center of the key, both looking for a pass from Ted. But Ted shot the ball instead. It clanged loudly against the rim, then bounced to the ground.

Alec picked it up and motioned for the boys to join him at center court.

"Okay. That drill was just a reminder that the best players know what their teammates' jobs are as well as their own. Something to keep in mind — especially next Saturday."

Alec smiled at the boys' puzzlement.

"What, didn't I tell you we're playing in our first scrimmage next week? The coach of the Benton Braves, another team in the league, called to see if we'd be ready for a non-league game. I told him we sure were!"

The boys buzzed excitedly. Then Cam Mullins piped up.

"But Coach, we don't even have a team name or uniforms yet! How can we play without those?"

But Alec had another surprise for them.

"Eight uniforms are on order. They're just waiting for us to give them a name. Any suggestions?"

Rusty thought hard. The other boys shouted out possibilities, like Tigers, Sharks, and Royals. But those names were either taken already or voted down. Then Rusty had an idea.

"How about the Lakers?" he suggested. "After all, Cato Lake is the only lake in this area, so who better than us to have that name?"

After a moment's thought, the boys all nodded.

It seemed like a good idea to everyone, including Alec Daws.

"Okay, enough of this chitchat! If we're really going to be ready to take on those Benton Braves, we'd better get some serious practicing in!"

The following Friday, each boy was presented with a new dark-blue-and-red team uniform. The name Lakers was emblazoned on the back along with a number. The next afternoon, each boy wore his uniform proudly for the scrimmage against the Benton Braves.

Rusty still couldn't quite believe that he was suited up with the others. After all, it was less than two weeks ago that he had persuaded his parents to let him play.

But a lot had happened since then. After giving himself his first insulin shot, Rusty found he was eager to continue. He realized how dependent he had been on his parents for that. And even though he still needed them to check the amount of insulin in the syringe, he knew they were proud of him for taking charge.

His playing had improved, too. More shots were going in, and he knew all the plays Alec had taught them as well as anyone else on the team.

Yet even with all these improvements on and off the court, Rusty was pretty sure he wouldn't be starting in the scrimmage against the Braves. After all, the other boys had been practicing together for a lot longer.

But as long as he got in the game at some point, Rusty knew he would be happy.

10

The Lakers looked sharp and eager in their blue-and-red uniforms. The Benton Braves were flashy in their green ones.

The game started. The Braves took the tap from center. They dribbled quickly and surely. Their passes were swift and accurate. Within thirty seconds they sank the first basket. Before the minute was up, they sank another.

Rusty watched the game from the bench. The Braves looked as courageous as their name suggested. By the end of the first quarter they were leading, 17 to 9.

And then he heard his name. He turned, his heart beating rapidly.

"Rusty! Report to the ref! Tell him you're going in in place of Mark!"

Rusty scrambled up and joined his teammates on the court. He was playing forward with Joey. Cam Mullins and Bud Farris played guard. Ted Stone was at center. He was taking Perry's place.

It was the Lakers' out near their own basket. Cam passed the ball from out of bounds to Bud. Bud dribbled a couple of steps and shot a quick pass to Joey, who was running toward the basket. Joey caught the ball and leapt. A Braves man jumped and slapped the ball, and it squirted from Joey's hands.

Rusty caught it!

What should I do with it? he thought, standing as if paralyzed. The ball had bounced to him unexpectedly.

"Shoot, Rusty! Shoot!" someone yelled.

He was near the corner, just about in the same position from where he had practiced taking shots on the court at home.

A Braves player bounded forward. He swung his arms wildly in front of Rusty. Rusty tried to feint to the left, then to the right. The player bobbed up and down in front of him like a puppet.

Rusty leapt as high as he could. He flipped the ball with his wrists toward the basket. It sailed in a high arc, struck the rim, and bounced up into the air. Then it dropped — right through the net!

A roar burst from the Lakers fans. "Thataboy, Rusty!"

Rusty's heart melted. All at once his fright was gone. He had done it. He had made his first basket in a real game. Well, *almost* a real game.

The Braves' ball. They moved it down-court quickly.

The Braves player shot a pass across the court. Another Braves player caught it, feinted Cam out of position, then broke fast for the basket. Just as he leapt to try a layup, Ted hit his wrist.

Freeeee-e-et!

"Two shots!" said the referee. He held up two fingers, Ted's number.

Ted shook his head, discouraged. He held up his hand to show he was the offender.

The Braves man sank the first shot, missed the second. Ted caught the rebound and zipped a pass to Bud. Bud dribbled the ball upcourt. He shot a bounce pass to Rusty. Rusty passed it back to him, then hurried to his corner spot. He hoped the ball would be passed to him. But his man guarded him well. No one dared to pass it.

Cam tried a set shot from the opposite corner. He missed. Ted and the Braves center leapt for the rebound. They both came down together with the ball gripped tightly in their hands.

Freeee-e-et! Jump ball.

A Braves man took the tap, then passed to a teammate. Once again the ball zipped in the other direction. Just as Rusty let out a sigh of disappointment, a player accidentally kicked his right foot. The player was Rusty's man. He stumbled forward, but hurriedly regained his balance.

The kick knocked Rusty off balance, too. Rusty fell. He struck the floor with his hip, then skidded and rolled over.

Again the whistle.

"Tripping!" shouted the referee, pointing at the Braves player. "You shoot one!" he said to Rusty.

The Braves players shouted something at the referee. They didn't like that call.

I wouldn't call that a foul, either, Rusty thought. It was an accident.

Rubbing his hip, he stepped to the free-throw line.

The referee waited till the players were ready on each side of the free-throw lane, then handed the ball to Rusty. "One shot," he repeated.

Nervously Rusty took the ball. He bounced it a few times, then looked long and carefully at the basket. A hush fell upon the big gym.

Rusty shot. The ball hit the rim, rolled around it, and fell off!

A half a dozen pairs of hands reached up for the rebound. Jim Bush got it. In the next instant someone knocked it out of his hands. It bounced across the floor. Rusty hurried after it and scooped it up. A tall, broad-shouldered Braves player reached it a moment later. He wrapped his arm around the ball and tried to whip it out of Rusty's hands.

Rusty held on as tightly as he could. The

Braves player was strong. He practically picked Rusty off his feet and swung him around the floor! Rusty fell, but he still held on to the ball. The Braves player bent on one knee beside Rusty and looked at him unbelievingly.

The Lakers fans roared out in laughter: "That's the boy, Rusty! Don't let him take it from you!"

Jump ball. The Braves player won his argument this time. He outjumped Rusty easily. Ten seconds later the Braves scored a basket. The buzzer sounded. Mark and Perry came back into the game. Rusty and Ted went out.

They sat on the bench beside Coach Alec Daws. Their faces glistened with perspiration.

"How do you feel, Rusty?" asked Alec.

Rusty's chest rose and fell as he breathed. "Okay!" he said.

Alec grinned. "You did fine," he said. "In the second half, we'll let you go in again."

Rusty grinned back. "I'll be ready!"

11

The score was 26–19, in favor of the Braves, as the second half started.

Rusty was impressed by Perry. He watched his every move. There was no doubt that Perry was the best player on the Lakers team — perhaps, at this moment, the best player on the floor.

Thoughts ran through Rusty's mind as he watched Perry catch passes, make fast breaks, and leap for layups. Perry went up high, as if he had springs in his legs.

He's so good, thought Rusty. I bet Alec

wishes he could have a whole team of Perrys.

Just then, Alec called out something that surprised Rusty.

"C'mon, Perry, heads up! Concentrate on the plays! Work the ball around more! Look for the open man, don't just shoot every time you get your hands on the ball!"

Rusty knew that teamwork and smart on-court thinking were as important to Alec as good passes and shots. Suddenly he wondered if Perry, who often ignored the plays to drive for the hoop or take impossible shots, really was the best player out there after all.

A loud cheer from the Lakers fans brought Rusty's thoughts back to the game. He saw Cam running up-court with a proud smile on his face and knew Cam must have sunk one.

The electric scoreboard flashed the score: VISITORS — 21; HOME — 26.

The gap was closing.

"Okay, Rusty," said Alec. "Go in the minute the ball is dead. Ted, in for Perry."

When he got into the game, he remembered Alec's words to Perry. He didn't want to do anything against Alec's wishes, anything that would give Alec a good reason not to let him play again.

Rusty concentrated on the play. When his part in it came, he was ready. The pass came fast.

It was from Ted Stone, who was being pressed by two Braves players.

Rusty caught the pass. A quick glance showed him he was the most open man on his team. So he aimed for the basket and shot.

In!

A thunderous roar sprang from the Lakers

fans. "Nice eye, Rusty! That's the way to sink 'em!"

Later, there was a scramble for the ball near him. It was impossible for him to get out of the way, so he tried for the ball himself. He was pushed, shoved, and almost got his hands on the ball. A quicker pair of hands snapped it up. Hands belonging to a Braves player.

Darn it! Rusty thought. I'll get it next time.

But he didn't have a chance. The quarter ended. Alec put Mark back into the game. Rusty sat out the last quarter, not caring whether he went in again or not. He was pooped. When the game ended, the shower was a welcome, joyful relief. No one was too unhappy that the Braves had won, 48–41. That was a better score than the Lakers had expected.

"You were great, Rusty!" said Joey as they rode home. "Man! How many sinkers?"

"Two field goals," said Cam. "Nothing wrong with that!"

Rusty blushed. It was good to hear his friends talk that way about him.

The *Cannerville News* printed a brief story about the game on Monday. It also had the box scores. Rusty read it over proudly.

	FG	FT	TP
C. Mullins g	2	1	5
B. Farris g	3	2	8
J. Bush g	0	0	0
J. Main f	1	1	3
M. Andrews f	4	0	8
R. Young f	2	0	4
P. Webb c	4	2	10
T. Stone c	1	1	3
	17	7	41

School ended the next week. The team practiced every day except Friday. On the Saturday after the Braves game, the Lakers played the Weston Jets, in their first official league game. The Jets beat them, 51 to 42. In that game Rusty sank only one basket.

"That was a big score," said Alec. "But not big when you hear what they've been doing to other teams. They beat the Braves, 48 to 22. And the Redwings, 43 to 19. So you see they have a strong defensive team. Yet we were able to go through them for 42 points! I think that's wonderful. You boys deserve a lot of credit."

On the Saturday before July Fourth, the Lakers played the Chilton Chiefs.

"Beat them and you'll have something to cheer about," said Alec. "They took the Braves to camp last week, 37 to 35."

The game was played on a high school court at Chilton. The seats were nearly filled as the game got under way.

Rusty wasn't surprised he didn't start. The Chiefs were supposed to be very strong. Perhaps he wouldn't see action in today's game at all.

Bud Farris plunked in the first basket of the game. The Lakers fans cheered him loudly. Then Perry stole a pass intended for a Chiefs player, broke fast for the basket, and laid it up!

Four points for the Lakers!

The Chiefs, dressed in crimson uniforms with large white numbers on their jerseys, grew cautious. They moved the ball slowly across the center line toward their basket. The Lakers used a zone defense and protected their goal closely.

Quickly a Chiefs player passed to a teammate at his left. The man broke forward. He leapt, holding the ball high over his head. Instead of shooting for a basket, he passed to another man rushing in. The man caught the pass and leapt for a jump shot.

In!

A few moments later, the Chiefs did it again. Gradually they crept ahead of the Lakers. Perry dumped in two long sets, and Cam Mullins a layup. The Lakers were trying hard, but the Chiefs had control of the game now. They led, 14 to 11, when the quarter ended.

Rusty started the second quarter in place of Mark Andrews. His heart raced as he took his position on the court.

He played the corner but was guarded so closely that he wasn't thrown a pass once during the first two minutes. Disgusted, he glanced toward the bench. Of course no one looked his way. He might as well sit down and watch the game as stand here like a store dummy.

"Rusty! Wake up!"

He turned just in time. A large blur popped up in front of him. He stuck out his hands and caught the bouncing ball. Like a swarm of angry hornets, the Chiefs players came after him. He feinted to the left and then to the right, using his left foot as a pivot.

Suddenly one of the players got hold of the ball. He yanked it hard. Rusty hung on desperately. If he couldn't shoot, nobody was going to take the ball from him, either.

Rusty was jerked forward. He fell, striking the floor hard with his right knee. Pain shot through it. A boy tripped over him as he did so, whacking Rusty on the shoulder. But Rusty still held firmly on to the ball.

The whistle shrilled.

"Jump!" said the referee.

Joey helped Rusty to his feet. "Nice going, pal. You okay?"

Rusty nodded.

The Chiefs player outjumped him. Another Chiefs man took the tap and dribbled downcourt.

Again the whistle. The referee signaled with his hands. Traveling. The ball returned to the Lakers.

The buzzer sounded. Mark Andrews came in. Rusty went out, limping.

Alec Daws looked sharply at Rusty. "You hung on to that ball like a dog with a bone," he said. "But just be sure you don't get hurt playing like that!"

Rusty sat down. "I couldn't *give* them the ball," he said. "Anyway, I didn't get hurt."

"Oh, no?" The coach's brows arched. "Then why are you limping?"

Rusty shrugged. He didn't answer that one. After all, what did Coach expect? Everybody fell sometime!

"Rusty, you're a scrappy, energetic player. But remember, just because your diabetes doesn't keep you out of the game doesn't mean a real injury won't sideline you. No one, least of all me, is going to think less of you if the other guy sometimes gets the ball. So play tough, but smart."

Rusty knew Alec was giving him good advice. But still, part of him knew the next time someone tried to swipe the ball, he'd hang on hard just as he had before.

He didn't want anyone to think he wasn't willing — or able — to give every play his all.

12

There was one minute left in the first half. The Cannerville Lakers were four points behind. They were gradually catching up to the Chiefs, thanks to Perry's layups.

Lakers' ball. Bud Farris had it. He dribbled across the center line — and fumbled! He fumbles so much! thought Rusty.

A Chiefs man scooped up the ball. Quickly Perry stole it from him! He shot a swift pass to Joey. Joey broke fast for the basket and shot the ball against the board. Missed!

"Ooooo!" wailed the fans.

A wild scramble followed for the rebound. Perry got it, then tapped it in!

Two points behind the Chiefs!

Chiefs' ball. They worked it to their back court. They tried to move into their front court, but couldn't. The Lakers had it well guarded.

They tried a set. The ball struck the backboard and missed the rim. Cam Mullins leapt, took the rebound, and dribbled all the way up the court. He was chased by five Chiefs players, but no one reached him in time. Cam leapt and made the layup, tying the score just as the half ended!

The Lakers rushed off happily to the locker room. Cheers from their fans trailed after them.

"You boys have improved wonderfully," Coach Daws said, his eyes beaming as he

faced the eight boys sitting on benches between the two rows of lockers. "It makes me
feel proud because, in a way, I'm a part of
you. You've come a long way in a short time.
You've learned to play the game very well.
You've listened to me and remembered a lot
of the things I've told you. More important
still, you're all good sports. Maybe — just
maybe — we might go home this afternoon
with a win!"

The second half went along with both
teams scoring freely. The electric scoreboard flashed a new score first on the home
side, and then on the visitors' side, seesaw-
ing back and forth.

With two minutes to play in the third
quarter, the coach had Rusty go in. Rusty
couldn't wait to get back out there. He
hadn't been sure the coach would let him
play again in this game.

Alec winked at him. "The right corner, Rusty. Let's see you dump in a couple."

Rusty took his position to the right of the basket and about five feet in from the out-of-bounds line. Nervously he watched the game as if he were a spectator.

Soon the action was on the Lakers' front court. Perry flipped a pass to Cam. Cam bounced the ball to Rusty, and Rusty shot.

Whack! A hand slapped his wrist. The whistle shrilled.

The ball missed the hoop by a foot, but Rusty was given two shots for a personal foul.

Carefully he aimed at the basket. Shot.

Made it!

He aimed again. Shot. Again he made it!

"Thataboy, Rus!" Cam yelled.

A little while later, the quarter ended. Rusty expected to be taken out. But he was still in as the fourth quarter got under way.

Action increased as the final minutes ticked away on the big clock above the scoreboard. Now the Chiefs were in the lead. Now the Lakers.

Rusty felt himself penned in. He wanted to join in the action. He felt good now. The pain from the fall had long since vanished. Gradually he crept farther and farther away from the corner.

Lakers' ball. Perry passed it to Rusty. Rusty turned, dribbled twice, then shot. The ball struck the backboard and sank for two points! At the same time, someone bumped into him, and a whistle pierced the gym.

"One shot!"

Rusty's face shone with perspiration as he stood on the free-throw line. His heart hammered as he took the ball from the referee. He aimed, shot.

In!

The fans roared. The Lakers were ahead now — 43 to 41. Rusty breathed hard. He had done a lot of running in the last few minutes.

With two minutes to go, he was taken out.

"Nice game, Rusty," said Alec.

Rusty looked at the coach. Alec's eyes were shining happily. Rusty smiled.

The Chiefs picked up another basket to tie the score. Then Mark arched in a set shot to put the Lakers ahead again. Five seconds before the finish of the game, Joey tried a long set shot, *made it*, and the game was over.

Score: Lakers — 47; Chiefs — 43.

There was a lot of singing in the cars as the boys rode home. And there was a lot to sing about. They had beaten the team that had whipped the Braves!

"No more games till after the July Fourth break," announced Alec Daws. "But don't let that stop you from practicing! Oh, and anyone who's around on the Fourth, stop by Cato Lake. I've got a surprise there!"

13

Rusty wondered what the surprise was, but he didn't ask. He didn't think Alec would tell him.

But by July Fourth, he was dying of curiosity. So when Marylou suggested the family head over to Cato Lake for an afternoon picnic, his heart leapt.

Rusty spotted Alec immediately. Alec waved to him to come over. Joey and Perry were already with him, all three of them splashing around in the refreshing water. Marylou came, too.

"You guys sit tight, and I'll go get the surprise," Alec said, his eyes dancing mischievously.

Five minutes later a colorful sailboat with a trim white sail skimmed across the water from the direction Alec had gone. So this was his surprise!

Alec sailed close to shore and called out, "Anybody interested in a ride?"

Perry was the first one to answer. "You bet! Permission to come aboard, sir?" He gave Alec a mock salute, then scrambled out of the water onto the boat's deck.

Laughing, Alec turned them away from the shore and out into the center of the lake.

After a while, they returned. Perry's eyes were shining with excitement.

"That was great!" he yelled as he jumped down.

Without hesitation, Joey took his place and again Alec's boat sped away from shore.

Rusty could hardly wait for his turn. When Joey and Alec came back, he clambered aboard the second Joey was off.

"First, put this on," said Alec, handing him a life preserver. "Rules of the boat."

Rusty felt bulky in the preserver, but once he and Alec were in the middle of the lake, he was glad he had it on. That water looked deep!

The wind picked up a bit. The sailboat tipped sharply to the left, and Rusty's heart jumped.

Alec grinned at him. "Don't worry!" he shouted. "We won't tip over!"

And sure enough, Alec straightened the boat out a moment later.

"How do you like it, Rusty?" Alec asked.

"It's great!" Rusty replied enthusiastically.

"I made it myself. As much as I love basketball, I love sailing, too. Now that the weather's warmer, I hope I can be out here every day!"

Too soon, Alec turned the boat back to shore. As they neared the water's edge, he gazed off to the left to something on the land. He kept looking, as if fascinated by some strange sight.

Suddenly a gust of wind tugged at the sail. It swung sharply right toward Rusty's head!

Alec quickly pulled it back before it could hit him.

"Whew!" said Rusty.

As Alec adjusted the boat's course, Rusty turned to see what had caught his attention so completely.

Then he grinned. Standing on shore, patiently waiting her turn, was Marylou.

Alec cleared his throat. "Think your sister would like a ride?" he whispered to Rusty.

"You'd better give her one or I won't hear the end of it!" Rusty whispered back.

When Marylou and Alec had sailed off, Perry snorted with disgust.

"Well, I guess that ends that," he said, looking at Rusty. "We might as well go home. Why'd you have to bring your sister, anyway?"

Rusty was stunned. "She's got as much right to be here as you do!" he retorted.

"Sure," said Perry. "Course, it won't hurt your playing time if she and Alec hit it off." He stared out at the sailboat. "I mean, if the coach is dating your sister, chances are you'll be in the starting lineup, right?"

14

Perry's unkind words rang in Rusty's ears the rest of the holiday weekend. So what if Alec and Marylou liked each other? Surely that wouldn't have anything to do with the team!

When the Lakers met for their next practice, Rusty decided to stay as far away from Perry as he could. But that proved to be impossible.

For only the second time since they'd started practicing under Alec's coaching, Rusty was in the starting lineup. He didn't have to look at Perry to know what he thought of that.

In the deepest, darkest part of his brain, Rusty wondered. Wondered if maybe Perry was right, if Alec had chosen him to start because of Marylou. That Marylou was in the stands right now made him even more uneasy.

Had he struggled to become a better player, to fight against his diabetes, only to find a place in the starting lineup thanks to his sister?

No one else on the team seemed to notice anything. Practice went along without a hitch — except that Rusty and Perry avoided each other as much as they could.

The next day it was the same thing all over again. By the end of that practice, Rusty realized that if he and Perry were going to be able to play as a team, he needed to know the truth. He cornered Alec as soon as he could.

"Yes, Rusty, what is it?" Alec asked. "You look like you're about to burst."

"Are you playing favorites because you like my sister?" Rusty blurted. "I mean, you didn't start me before you took Marylou for a sailboat ride!"

Alec frowned. "I wouldn't be a very good coach if I pulled something like that, would I? I'm starting you because I think you're the best man for the job." He put a hand on Rusty's shoulder. "And you can tell Perry I said that."

Rusty's head shot up. "You knew?"

"That Perry's the one who put that idea in your head? I'd have to be blind not to see that you two haven't been getting along this week. But let me tell you this, Rusty: If I have any doubts that you two won't play well together against Bay Town, a very tough team, I won't hesitate to replace one of you. You can tell Perry I said *that*, too."

Suddenly, though, Rusty felt a weight lift from his shoulders. Perry had been wrong, but that didn't make Rusty's attitude toward him this week right. He should have cleared the air long ago — and he meant to do so as soon as possible.

"Thanks, Alec," he said. "I'm going to talk to Perry right now!"

Rusty caught up to Perry a minute or two later. Perry turned in surprise when he heard Rusty call his name.

His eyes darkened as he listened to Rusty. When Rusty was done, he said angrily, "I can't believe you ratted about me to Alec!"

But Rusty wasn't about to trade one argument for another. "Perry, for the good of the team, we have to get this worked out. Why can't you just accept that I'm a good enough player to be on the starting lineup?"

Perry didn't answer right away. Then he blurted it out. "You've got a disease, that's why! And I've seen what happens to you when you get sick! What if it happens on the court during an important game?"

Rusty's stomach tightened. He had no reply. After all, he couldn't assure Perry that what he feared wouldn't happen. It could.

And no one knew better than Rusty did how bad that would be.

15

Bay Town was as strong that following Saturday as Alec had said it would be. Their center, a slim, blond boy who jumped, dribbled, and passed with equal skill, was taller than Perry. Rusty could tell that this kid was practically Bay Town's team. Without him, they'd be nothing.

At the end of the first quarter, the score was Bay Town — 11; Lakers — 4.

"Perry, you, Joey, and Bud cover that star center on defense," advised Alec. "Try to keep him from scoring. That'll be our only chance."

In the second quarter, the boys clung to the tall Bay Town center like leeches. They held him to two baskets. The Lakers scored seventeen points. The score at the end of the first half: Bay Town — 15; Lakers — 21.

In the second half, the Bay Towners were a confused bunch of boys. The blond center tried steadily to get away from his guards but had little luck. Perry fouled him twice. And Cam did, too. Other than that, the center scored very few points. Meanwhile, the Lakers were dumping them in.

Rusty played his share of the game. From the corner he sank three set shots. He was fouled three times. He sank two of his free throws, for a total of eight points.

He had played a good game. He wished his parents were here to see him.

The Lakers carried home the win, 48–36.

It was a shocking loss to Bay Town. A fine team like theirs losing to a bunch of boys who had never played under a coach's guidance before this year? Impossible!

But it had happened!

Thanks to that win, the Cannerville Lakers were ready to face their toughest opponents yet. Alec printed a sign and hung it in the store. It read:

> **Basketball Game**
> **Lakers vs. Culbert**
> **Saturday, July 18, 2 p.m.**
> **at the Culbert Junior High Gym**
> **Everybody come!**
> **Cheer your local team on to victory!**

The sign stirred up interest. Soon the game was the talk of the town.

"We'll have a crowd there for sure!" said Perry Webb excitedly.

"We probably will," replied Cam. "But what will they think of us if we lose?"

"Won't be any disgrace," said Alec. "Everybody knows that Culbert was runner-up for the championship last year. Our fans won't boo our team if it loses to a team like Culbert. But let's get this losing idea out of our heads! Let's think of *winning,* not *losing!*"

On Tuesday, Wednesday, and Thursday afternoons, Alec worked hard with the boys. There were a few things most of them still did not do well. Cam still was unable to get his passes away fast enough. Joey still couldn't sink more than one out of eight from the foul line. Bud's dribbling had improved. So had his passes. But he still fumbled the ball a lot. And when he did, he always seemed to be near an opponent. And Ted, Perry, Rusty — they all needed improvement as well.

Alec put in a few minutes of practice himself. It was fun to watch him. He hardly used his injured hand. His other one was all he needed. He dribbled swiftly and gracefully. When he jumped to sink a layup, his feet lifted high off the floor. His hand seemed to go almost higher than the rim. When he finished playing, perspiration glistened on his face, but you could tell he enjoyed those moments with all his heart.

He probably could have been a great basketball player, thought Rusty. Such thoughts made him all the more grateful for the chance Alec and his parents had given him to play. Grateful, and determined to succeed.

❁　　　❁　　　❁

The Culbert Junior High gym was packed that Saturday afternoon. Many fans from Cannerville came to see the game and give their boys support.

Perry and the Culbert center went up on the jump ball. Perry's long fingers tapped it. Bud caught it, dribbled away, and fumbled!

Culbert scooped up the fumble. A pass downcourt. A quick dribble. Then a layup.

In! Two points for Culbert, and the game was hardly ten seconds old!

Lakers' out. Perry took the pass from Joey and dribbled the ball up-court. He crossed the center line. A Culbert player tried to slap the ball away from him. Perry passed to Cam. Joey started toward the right-hand corner, then came forward quickly under the basket. Cam bounced the ball under his guard's arm to Joey. Joey took it, leapt, and tried a hook shot.

In!

Rusty grinned at his friend as they beat it downcourt to play defense.

Culbert's out. A long pass downcourt. A Culbert player was there to catch it. He dribbled it toward his basket, then leapt for the layup. Missed!

Perry was right behind him. He caught the rebound and brought the ball back up-court. Carefully he passed to Joey. Joey passed to Rusty. The five of them ran back and forth in a weaving pattern in the back court. Each looked for a chance for a fast break. But Culbert guarded their basket like a family of lions guarding their cub.

Then Perry faked a pass to Bud, throwing his man off guard. He was at least ten feet away from the basket. He took quick aim and shot. The ball arced, fell through the rim, and rippled the net for two points!

A yell broke from the Lakers fans. What a clean, beautiful shot!

The Lakers had been tight as banjo strings when the game had started. They had moved about like wooden puppets. Now, as the first quarter drew to a close, they were no longer stiff and nervous. They moved with better timing. They were more careful with their throws.

Tension was growing, interest mounting. Was this the Culbert team that had finished second in last year's championship? Was this the team that almost everybody had thought would beat a little nobody like the Lakers with their hands tied behind their backs?

What had happened to their great power?

And what of the Lakers — was this really a *nobody* team?

16

When the buzzer sounded, ending the first quarter, every fan in the gym knew that the Lakers were *somebody*, indeed!

"Boys," Alec said while they dried the perspiration from their shoulders and faces, "you're playing wonderful ball. Keep it up, and we'll leave this town gasping for breath. I heard several of these Culbert fans call us hicks." He smiled. "I think I've already heard their teeth crunching, eating their own words!"

At the start of the second quarter, the lineup was Cam and Bud at guard, Rusty and Joey at forward, and Perry at center. They felt ready.

But Culbert started off with fast breaks. They took the Lakers by surprise for a while, sinking two layups in quick succession.

"Come on!" cried Perry. "Let's crush that charge!"

Perry's spark encouraged his four teammates to put on more fire. They not only crushed Culbert's charge; they also breezed past them.

When four minutes of the second quarter were up, the scoreboard read: VISITORS — 19; HOME — 14.

Many Culbert fans, looking at the score, could hardly believe it was their team trailing in the game.

Then, suddenly, the play was near Rusty. Joey had the ball. He couldn't pass it to anyone else. He had to pass it to Rusty.

"Shoot, Rusty!" he said.

Rusty almost missed the pass. The ball struck his fingers. It hurt the middle finger of his right hand. He moved into position to throw. Just as he flipped the ball, a boy jumped in front of him and struck his hand!

Shreee-e-ek!

"Foul!" yelled the referee. "Number five! Two shots!"

The Lakers fans cheered Rusty as he walked slowly to the free-throw line. The noise quieted down. The referee gave Rusty the ball. Rusty took his time, aimed, and shot.

In!

One more to go. Again he aimed and carefully shot.

In!

The score now: 21–14. The Lakers were really moving!

The buzzer. Culbert sent in subs. Two tall boys.

"Uh-oh," murmured Rusty. "What's this?"

Culbert's out. They moved the ball swiftly downcourt. The tall boys were doing most of the moving. They passed the ball quickly, accurately. A moment later one of them rushed forward, took a pass, leapt.

A layup!

The Lakers' out. They dribbled up-court, crossed the center line. Then someone rushed in, intercepted a pass, and dribbled downcourt! Another basket!

Alec called a time-out. On the sidelines, Rusty was breathing heavily and sweating hard. Alec looked at him closely, then told Mark to sub in at forward.

Rusty sank onto the bench as play resumed. Although *he* knew he was just tired, Alec's glance had told him Alec was worried

he might be having trouble with his diabetes.

Suddenly Rusty had a vision of what it
would be like if he *did* have an insulin reaction on the court. It would stop the game —
and end his career with the team.

All at once, Rusty was grateful to Alec for
looking out for him. He turned his attention
to the game.

The electric clock on the wall ticked on.
The Lakers put in another basket, but Culbert sank three to the Lakers' one. The half
ended with a change on the scoreboard: VIS-
ITORS — 23; HOME — 24.

Culbert was coming back!

17

They held their big guns out on us," said Coach Alec Daws. "Somebody has to stop them, or we'll get smeared, surely."

They were resting in the coolness of the locker room during halftime. No one had any comment.

Alec walked back and forth between the rows of benches, thinking. Then he looked up.

"There is a way to stop those tall boys from dunking those baskets," he said suddenly. "Joey, you and Bud cover the dark-haired one. I noticed that he's the better shot of the two. Perry, you stay with the blond. I think you can handle him. Press him a little closer, but watch yourself. We can't afford fouls. Cam and Mark, cover the other three. Anyway, we'll see how this strategy works."

The second half soon started. The tall, dark-haired Culbert player took the tap. Joey and Bud swarmed around him like a couple of bothersome bees. He finally passed off.

Mark intercepted the ball! He dribbled downcourt, then passed to Perry. Perry's guard was suddenly beside him. Perry stopped, passed to Bud. Bud leapt for a layup.

A bucket!

The Lakers fans roared.

Culbert realized what the Lakers were

doing. The tall boys put on more speed to try to shake off their guards. Culbert's three smaller players began to handle the ball more often. They took more shots. Most of them were careless ones. They missed the rim completely. But some throws found their mark. The Lakers sank one occasionally, too, but the score was going ahead in favor of Culbert.

It looks as if I'm stuck here on the bench, thought Rusty. I can sink them from the corner. Both corners! I'm sure I can! Didn't I sink nine out of ten during practice Thursday night? And on Wednesday, didn't I sink twelve out of fifteen? Isn't that something Alec should think about?

The score at the end of the third quarter was Culbert — 33; Lakers — 30.

"Rusty, take Mark's place this quarter," said Alec.

Rusty leapt up as if he'd been shot out of a cannon. "Yes, sir!" he said.

He reported to the referee. At the start of the quarter, he shook hands with his man, then played his usual position.

Culbert's tall blond got away from Perry, dribbled all the way down the court, and laid one up. That put them five points ahead of the Lakers.

"Come on, Lakers!" the fans shouted. "Get in there and play ball!"

Lakers' out. They played cautiously. Each pass was carefully made. They could not take a chance of interception.

Rusty crept out of the corner. He swung in behind Perry, took the pass from him, and started to shoot. A quick hand slapped the ball down. It bounced high. Rusty went after it, grabbed it, and dribbled toward the corner.

He turned. A man was coming toward him. Rusty shot quickly. The ball struck the inside of the rim and plunged through the net!

Two points!

"Thataway, Rus!" cried Perry.

The cry took Rusty completely by surprise. But the look Perry gave him spoke even louder than that. Rusty could see in an instant that Perry finally realized Rusty had earned his place on the team — and that his diabetes wasn't about to slow him down!

A few moments later, Perry intercepted a pass intended for the tall blond he was guarding. The ball zipped from one pair of hands to another. Finally Perry took the short pass beneath the basket. He went up and flipped the ball against the board.

Basket!

Culbert called time.

The Lakers didn't mind. They could use a two-minute rest.

18

Time in. Culbert's out. The tall boys had been taken out, replaced by smaller boys. They were fresh, eager. Culbert began to roll.

Fast dribbling. Quick passes. They sank two long set shots that drew a tremendous applause from the crowd.

The buzzer. Time out for the Lakers.

"Screen Rusty!" said Alec. "Give him some shots!"

Had Alec remembered those nights Rusty had dunked nine out of ten? And twelve out of fifteen?

Culbert played a man-to-man defense. But Jim Bush, playing in place of Joey, managed to slip a pass to Rusty. Then Jim got in front of Rusty to give him a screen. Rusty aimed, shot.

Basket!

Later, Perry made the same play. He screened Rusty, and again Rusty sank the shot.

"Good eye!" Perry praised him.

The Lakers now trailed by just one point — 39 to 38.

Time was called. The two tall boys returned to the game for Culbert.

"Rusty! Cam! Cover that one! I'll cover the blond!" yelled Perry.

In spite of Rusty's and Cam's efforts, the tall dark-haired forward for Culbert took a pass, broke fast for the basket, and dunked a layup.

Seconds later Cam sank a long one.

Culbert — 41; Lakers — 40.

Culbert's out. The tall blond took the pass from out of bounds and dribbled it up-court.

Swiftly Rusty ran forward, reached out his hand, and *stole the ball!*

He turned and dribbled downcourt — and felt as if weights were holding down his legs. A moment ago the clock had said only seconds to play. If he could get past the center line, well within throwing distance of the basket, he might be able to dump it in. If . . .

He crossed the center line. Culbert players sprang in front of him from both sides. Rusty stopped, aimed briefly, and shot. Just as he did so, one of the defenders leapt forward and struck Rusty's arm! He fell against Rusty, and both of them toppled hard to the floor.

Rusty was stunned. He couldn't get up. Time was called, and Alec hurried forward from the bench.

He crouched beside Rusty. "Rusty! Where did you get hurt?"

"My head," murmured Rusty. "I — I'll be all right. Just banged it a little."

The dizziness cleared. Alec helped him to his feet.

"You sure?" Alec said seriously. "You sure you really want to keep playing?"

Rusty cracked a smile. "I'm sure, Coach. I'm all right now. Honest!"

Alec grinned and slapped him on the shoulder. "Okay! You've got two foul shots coming. Let's see you make them both!"

Rusty stepped to the free-throw line. The referee handed him the ball. The gym was silent as Rusty took aim and shot.

In! The ball fell through the rim without touching it.

"This is it, Rus," said Perry near him. "Make it, and we're ahead!"

Rusty aimed carefully. He was nervous now. Boy, he was nervous!

He shot. The ball struck the rim, wobbled slightly, then dropped through the net!

"Perfect!" cried Perry.

The Lakers fans roared so loudly the place shook.

Ten seconds to go . . . nine . . . eight . . .

Culbert tried to move the ball as quickly as possible up-court. The Lakers were on them like hornets. Once . . . twice . . . the Lakers knocked down passes. Both times Culbert recovered the ball.

Seven . . . six . . . five . . .

Culbert's tall blond had the ball. He charged forward. Perry and Rusty both were in his way. The blond stopped. He feinted in different directions with the ball as Perry and Rusty got closer and closer to him.

Then he shot. It was a hurried throw. It missed the basket by inches.

Perry turned and ran back for the rebound just as the horn blew.

The game was over. The Lakers were the winners — 42 to 41.

Cheers filled the gym. Cheers from the Lakers fans.

"Here's the guy who won it for us!" Perry cried. "Come on, fellas! Let's give him a lift off the court!"

Before he knew what was happening, Rusty's teammates had put him on their shoulders and carried him off the floor.

Rusty heard a voice start singing behind him, and then everyone joined in:

For he's a jolly good fellow!
For he's a jolly good fellow!
For he's a jolly good fellow!
That nobody can deny!

Not only were the players singing; the Lakers fans were, too.

Rusty turned and met Alec's eyes squarely. Alec winked. There was no mistaking the happiness in his face. Rusty knew it was because Alec, who could never play basketball again himself, had turned a group of boys into a great basketball team.

That nobody can deny!
That nobody can deny!
For he's a jolly good fellow!
That nobody can deny!

The #1
Sports Series
for Kids

MATT CHRISTOPHER

Read them all!

Baseball Pals

Baseball Turnaround

The Basket Counts

Catch That Pass!

Catcher with a Glass Arm

Center Court Sting

Challenge at Second Base

The Comeback Challenge

Cool as Ice

The Counterfeit Tackle

Crackerjack Halfback

The Diamond Champs

Dirt Bike Racer

Dirt Bike Runaway

Double Play at Short

Face-Off

Football Fugitive

The Fox Steals Home

The Great Quarterback Switch

The Hockey Machine

Ice Magic

Inline Skater

Johnny Long Legs

The Kid Who Only Hit Homers

Long-Arm Quarterback

Long Shot for Paul

Look Who's Playing First Base

Miracle at the Plate

Mountain Bike Mania

No Arm in Left Field

Olympic Dream

Penalty Shot

Pressure Play

Prime-Time Pitcher

Red-Hot Hightops

The Reluctant Pitcher

Return of the Home Run Kid

Roller Hockey Radicals

Run, Billy, Run

Shoot for the Hoop

Shortstop from Tokyo

Skateboard Renegade

Skateboard Tough

Snowboard Maverick

Snowboard Showdown

Soccer Duel

Soccer Halfback

Soccer Scoop

Spike It!

The Submarine Pitch

Supercharged Infield

The Team That Couldn't Lose

Tennis Ace

Tight End

Too Hot to Handle

Top Wing

Touchdown for Tommy

Tough to Tackle

Wheel Wizards

Wingman on Ice

The Year Mom Won the Pennant

All available in paperback from Little, Brown and Company

Matt Christopher

Sports Bio Bookshelf

Kobe Bryant

Terrell Davis

John Elway

Julie Foudy

Jeff Gordon

Wayne Gretzky

Ken Griffey Jr.

Mia Hamm

Tony Hawk

Grant Hill

Derek Jeter

Randy Johnson

Michael Jordan

Lisa Leslie

Tara Lipinski

Mark McGwire

Greg Maddux

Hakeem Olajuwon

Briana Scurry

Sammy Sosa

Tiger Woods

Steve Young